D

D1621185

NORMAN
PRICE

BELLA
LASAGNE

JAMES

SARAH

# MEET ALL THESE FRIENDS IN BUZZ BOOKS:

Thomas the Tank Engine
The Animals of Farthing Wood
James Bond Junior
Fireman Sam
Joshua Jones
Rupert
Babar

First published in Great Britain by Buzz Books,
an imprint of Reed Children's Books
Michelin House, 81 Fulham Road, London SW3 6RB
and Auckland, Melbourne, Singapore and Toronto

ISBN 1 85591 322 4

Printed in Italy by Olivotto

# PRACTICE MAKES PERFECT

Story by Rob Lee
Illustrations by The County Studio

Station Officer Steele had set up a practice drill for the Pontypandy Fire Brigade, and he had asked Firefighter Penny Morris to come from nearby Newtown to observe the drill. She arrived at the fire station just in time for breakfast.

"You're going to be watching the pride of Pontypandy in action," boasted Firefighter Elvis Cridlington.

Elvis enjoyed showing off for Penny.

"Watch this," he said, cracking an egg.

The egg was meant to go into the frying
pan, but instead it landed on Elvis's boot!

Fireman Sam laughed. "I hope our drill is
more successful than your eggs, Elvis!"

"Oh no. I'm afraid that was the last egg,
Penny," said Elvis.

"Don't worry, Elvis," said Penny quickly.
"I've already eaten breakfast anyway."

After breakfast, Fireman Sam, Elvis and
Penny met Station Officer Steele in the
forecourt of the fire station.

"Newtown Fire Brigade will take any
emergency calls from Pontypandy during
the drill," Penny told Station Officer Steele.

"Good," he replied. "We're ready, then."

"What's the drill about, Sir?" asked Elvis.

"You'll find out in good time. A good fire
brigade must be ready for any emergency,"
said Station Officer Steele. He held up his
stopwatch. "Remember, I'll be timing you
from the moment that alarm goes off."

Just then, the alarm sounded.

Fireman Sam raced to the telex machine.
"There's been an accident at the quarry,"
he called to the others. "Let's go!"

The Pontypandy Fire Brigade sped out of the station. Soon they were racing through the countryside. When they arrived, Sam parked Jupiter in a field at the quarry's edge.

The practice dummy was lying at the bottom of the quarry.

"We'll need the ropes and the stretcher for this rescue, Elvis," said Sam.

He strapped himself into the harness, then Elvis lowered him into the quarry to the dummy below. Carefully, Sam secured the dummy onto the stretcher.

"Hoist away, Elvis," he shouted.

Slowly and steadily, Elvis pulled the rope until Fireman Sam and the stretcher had reached the top of the cliff.

"Well done, Elvis," said Sam, as he stepped out of the harness.

"Yes, well done, both of you," said Penny. "In a real rescue, the ambulance would be here to take the patient to hospital. But as our patient is a dummy, he can go in the truck with the rest of the equipment. Let's get back to the station as fast as we can!"

"You're making very good time," said Penny later, as they roared through the country lanes towards Pontypandy.

"Perhaps we'll even break the record for fastest practice drill!" exclaimed Elvis.

Suddenly, a rabbit dashed across the road in front of them, followed by Farmer Morgan's dog, Patch.

"Great fires of London!" cried Sam, as he
wrenched at the steering wheel.

Jupiter swerved off the road and slid
down an embankment into a tree. The
engine coughed and spluttered, then
conked out completely with a loud hiss.

"Is everybody all right?" asked Sam,
straightening his helmet.

14

"It's a good job we had our safety belts on," said Penny, looking at the others. "We're all fine, but I don't think Jupiter is too healthy."

Elvis climbed out of the engine, followed by Penny and Sam. A barking sound was coming from the fields. Elvis followed the noise to a steep ditch.

"Patch!" he exclaimed. "What are you doing down there?"

"Sam, Penny, come quick!" called Elvis.

Fireman Sam and Penny hurried over.

"Poor Patch," said Sam, when he saw the dog at the bottom of the ditch. "Luckily, he can't be hurt too badly or he wouldn't be leaping about so much. We'll use a harness to rescue him instead of the stretcher."

"I'll rescue him," Elvis volunteered.

Quickly, the firefighters set up the rescue
equipment, then Penny and Sam lowered
Elvis into the ditch.

Patch was so pleased to see Elvis that he
jumped into his arms, knocking him
backwards into the mud.

"Calm down, boy," said Elvis. "I can't
rescue you if you keep jumping on me!"

Finally, Elvis managed to get to his feet. He picked up Patch, and strapped the dog into the harness.

"Okay," he called.

Sam and Penny hoisted Patch to the surface and then pulled up Elvis.

19

Penny held Patch still while Fireman Sam examined him. Elvis went to get the first aid kit from Jupiter.

"Is Patch all right, Sam?" asked Elvis.

"He's hurt his paw," Sam replied.

Carefully, Sam wrapped a bandage around the injured paw. Patch whimpered softly.

"You'll be all right, Patch," said Sam. "A trip to the vet with Farmer Morgan, and I guarantee you'll be as good as new."

Patch barked and pranced about, holding his bandaged paw delicately in the air.

"I'll take Patch home," said Fireman Sam.

"Farmer Morgan will be wondering where he is," said Penny.

Fireman Sam and Patch set off together across the field.

While Sam was gone, Penny and Elvis tried
to fix Jupiter's engine with the tools from
the equipment locker.

"It's no use," said Penny. "We can't fix
Jupiter without spare parts."

"But we're miles away from the fire
station," said Elvis. "How will we get back?"

"I'm back!" called Sam.

Penny and Elvis looked up to see Sam driving towards them in a tractor.

"Farmer Morgan was so pleased we rescued Patch that he lent me his tractor to tow Jupiter home," explained Sam. "If we hurry, we can be back at the station in time for tea!"

Outside the fire station, Station Officer Steele was pacing up and down the forecourt and glaring at his stopwatch.

"At this rate the Pontypandy Fire Brigade will set the record for the WORST drill time ever!" he muttered. "I could have done it quicker with an old-fashioned horse-drawn fire engine."

24

Just then Fireman Sam chugged into
view on the tractor, merrily towing Jupiter
towards the station.

"Good grief!" gasped Station Officer
Steele, but he listened closely as Fireman
Sam explained what had happened.

"Well," Station Officer Steele said at last,
"in that case, you've all done a superb job."

Once Fireman Sam had unhooked the towing cables, Penny and Elvis set to work repairing Jupiter's engine. They found the spare parts they needed in the storeroom.

"I'd better return the tractor," said Fireman Sam. "I won't be long. Farmer Morgan said he would give me a lift back."

"Can you collect some more eggs while you're at Morgan's Farm?" asked Elvis.

"Good idea," Sam replied. He climbed aboard the tractor and drove off.

"That should fix it," said Penny later,
shutting Jupiter's bonnet. "Start the
engine, Elvis."

Elvis turned the key. Jupiter sprang to life!

"Well done!" exclaimed Station Officer
Steele. "Now Jupiter is ready for the next
practice drill."

Elvis groaned.

Elvis, Penny and Station Officer Steele were
in the mess when Fireman Sam arrived
carrying a large crate.

"What have you got there?" asked Elvis.

Suddenly, something in the box clucked.

Fireman Sam opened the box and lifted
out a very noisy chicken.

"I'd like you to meet Hilda the hen,"
said Fireman Sam with a smile. "Now
we'll never run out of eggs!"

FIREMAN SAM

STATION OFFICER
STEELE

TREVOR EVANS

ELVIS
CRIDLINGTON